YASMIN

The Camper

written by
SAADIA FARUQI

illustrated by
HATEM ALY

PICTURE WINDOW BOOKS
a capstone imprint

To Mariam for inspiring me, and Mubashir
for helping me find the right words—S.F.

To my sister, Eman, and her amazing girls,
Jana and Kenzi—H.A.

Published by Picture Window Books, an imprint of Capstone
1710 Roe Crest Drive
North Mankato, Minnesota 56003
capstonepub.com

Text copyright © 2024 by Saadia Faruqi.
Illustrations copyright © 2024 by Capstone.

Library of Congress Cataloging-in-Publication Data
Names: Faruqi, Saadia, author. | Aly, Hatem, illustrator. | Faruqi, Saadia.
Yasmin. Title: Yasmin the camper / written by Saadia Faruqi ; illustrated
by Hatem Aly.
Description: North Mankato, Minnesota : Picture Window Books, an
imprint of Capstone, [2024] | Series: Yasmin | Audience: Ages 5-8. |
Audience: Grades K-1. | Summary: Yasmin is excited but nervous about
her first camping trip with her scout troop—and a tent that threatens to
collapse does not help.
Identifiers: LCCN 2023021068 (print) | LCCN 2023021069 (ebook) |
   ISBN 9781666393934 (hardcover) | ISBN 9781484696347 (paperback) |
   ISBN 9781484696354 (pdf) | ISBN 9781484696361 (epub)
Subjects: LCSH: Muslim girls—Juvenile fiction. | Pakistani Americans—
Juvenile fiction. | Camping—Juvenile fiction. | Self-confidence—Juvenile
fiction. | CYAC: Pakistani Americans—Fiction. | Camping—Fiction. |
Self-confidence—Fiction. | LCGFT: Picture books.
Classification: LCC PZ7.1.F373 Yav 2024 (print) | LCC PZ7.1.F373 (ebook)
| DDC 813.6 [Fic]—dc23/eng/20230620
LC record available at https://lccn.loc.gov/2023021068
LC ebook record available at https://lccn.loc.gov/2023021069

Designer: Sarah Bennett

Design Elements: Shutterstock/LiukasArt

TABLE OF CONTENTS

CHAPTER ONE

Going Camping

Yasmin's scout troop was taking their first camping trip. Yasmin was excited but also a little worried. She'd never been camping before.

"Goodbye, jaan," Baba said as he hugged Yasmin. "Remember, you can do anything you set your mind to!"

"Ready for an adventure?"
Emma's mom, Mrs. Winters,
asked.

The scouts nodded. "Ready!"
They headed up a path into
the trees. "What do you notice?"
Mrs. Winters asked.

"It's quiet," Yasmin said. "No cars honking. Nobody yelling."

Mrs. Winters smiled. "Yes, we're far from the city."

And far from my family, Yasmin thought nervously.

Then they heard birds chirping.

"That's the kind of noise we like to hear," Mrs. Winters said. "Take out your sketchbooks, please!"

The scouts sat near some big trees. Yasmin saw a red cardinal and a blue jay. Emma pointed out three blackbirds. Yasmin drew a picture for Mama and Baba.

CHAPTER TWO

Collapsing Tent

Next Mrs. Winters led the troop to a creek.

"We'll set up camp here," she said.

"I can't wait to sleep in our tent!" Emma said.

Yasmin didn't say anything.

She wanted to sleep in a
tent too. But Mama wouldn't be
there to tuck her in. What if she
couldn't sleep? What if she got
scared and wanted to go home?

The scouts played near the creek. They found pretty rocks and even saw some tiny fish. Yasmin tried to forget her worries.

"Gather round, scouts!" Mrs. Winters called. She showed them how to put up a tent. It looked easy.

Yasmin and Emma followed
the instructions.

They laid out their tent. They
slid the poles into the flaps. They
put the stakes in the ground.

Yasmin and Emma looked at the tent when they were done.

"Why is it drooping?" Emma asked.

They adjusted the stakes. That didn't help. They pulled on the sides. That didn't help.

Yasmin began to worry again.
What if the tent fell on top of
them while they were sleeping?

She thought of her cozy bed
at home. She missed Mama and
Baba more than ever.

CHAPTER THREE

Sky Full of Stars

Yasmin took a deep breath.

She remembered what Baba had

told her: "You can do anything!"

She studied the tent. She tilted

her head to one side. She saw

that one of the pole flaps was

empty. "We're missing a pole!"

Yasmin said.

Emma looked inside the

tent bag and shook her head.

No pole.

Yasmin remembered the birds

on the tree branches. "I'll be

right back!" she shouted.

She ran over to the trees and
found lots of branches on the
ground. Some were too short.
Others were too crooked. Then she
found the perfect one. Long and
straight—just like a tent pole!

Yasmin brought it back to the

tent and slid it into the empty

flap. The tent stood up straight.

"Hooray!" Emma cried.

"Good problem solving,

Yasmin!" Mrs. Winters said.

Yasmin grinned.

When the sun set, they ate
soup and cornbread. Then they
roasted marshmallows over the
fire. Mrs. Winters pointed out the
stars in the sky.

Yasmin was having so much fun, she forgot all about missing Mama and Baba . . . almost.

"Isn't this great?" Emma whispered.

Yasmin nodded. Camping was great. And going home tomorrow would be great too!

Think About It, Talk About It

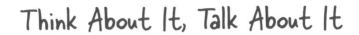

❇ Yasmin is both excited and nervous about camping. Think about a time you had two different feelings about something. What was that like?

❇ Yasmin misses Mama and Baba, but she doesn't tell anyone. Do you think it might have helped Yasmin to talk about her worries with others? What would you say to a friend who is feeling homesick?

❇ When Yasmin remembers what her baba told her, she feels "empowered." That means believing in oneself and having confidence. How did this feeling help Yasmin solve the tent problem?

Write About It

❄ Imagine you are going on an overnight camping trip. Write a list of all the things you think you should take along. Would all the items fit in your backpack?

❄ What if the tent DID collapse on Yasmin and Emma while they slept? Write a different ending to this story. What happened in the night, and what did Yasmin and Emma do?

❄ Have you ever seen a cardinal, a blue jay, or a blackbird, like Yasmin saw? Get out some paper and colored pencils and draw a bird that you have seen in your neighborhood.

Learn Urdu with Yasmin!

Yasmin's family speaks both English and Urdu. Urdu is a language from Pakistan. Maybe you already know some Urdu words!

baba (BAH-bah)—father

hijab (HEE-jahb)—scarf covering the hair

jaan (jahn)—life; a sweet nickname for a loved one

kameez (kuh-MEEZ)—long tunic or shirt

kitaab (keh-TAB)—book

nana (NAH-nah)—grandfather on mother's side

nani (NAH-nee)—grandmother on mother's side

salaam (sah-LAHM)—hello

shabash (shaa-BAASH)—well done

shukriya (shuh-KREE-yuh)—thank you

Make a Pine Cone Bird Feeder!

SUPPLIES:

- a pine cone
- string
- a butter knife
- nut butter (not sugar-free kind)
- birdseed
- a plate or pie pan

STEPS:

1. Tie the string around the pine cone and leave enough length to tie the other end to a tree branch.

2. Spread nut butter on the pine cone.

3. Pour birdseed onto the plate or pan and roll the pine cone in the seeds to coat it.

4. Hang your feeder from a tree and watch for birds to visit!

Saadia Faruqi is a Pakistani American writer, interfaith activist, and cultural sensitivity trainer featured in *O, The Oprah Magazine*. She also writes middle grade novels, such as *Yusuf Azeem Is Not a Hero*, and other books for children. Saadia is editor-in-chief of *Blue Minaret*, an online magazine of poetry, short stories, and art. Besides writing books, she also loves reading, binge-watching her favorite shows, and taking naps. She lives in Houston, Texas, with her family.

Hatem Aly is an Egyptian-born illustrator whose work has been featured in multiple publications worldwide. He currently lives in beautiful New Brunswick, Canada, with his wife, son, and more pets than people. When he is not dipping cookies in a cup of tea or staring at blank pieces of paper, he is usually drawing books. One of the books he illustrated is *The Inquisitor's Tale* by Adam Gidwitz, which won a Newbery Honor and other awards, despite Hatem's drawings of a farting dragon, a two-headed cat, and stinky cheese.

Join Yasmin on more adventures!

   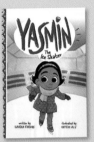

  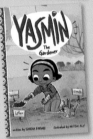